Preface

The two heroes of the epic clashed with each other three times during their lifetimes. This book is a compilation of ten pieces in poetic form bringing the details of those encounters to you.

THE WARRIOR PRINCE

born in a warrior family
he was destined
to be a king

the truth he could never shy away
the expectation he could never get away
he had taken all that in his stride
and carried the misery
with all his pride

training with weapons
and duelling with others
was how he spent the childhood
he never had a moment to rest
as he always strived to be the best

all the hard work had come to fruition
he was now a young man
majestic and magnificent

a tempest about to break through
almost like a prophecy
waiting to come true

when he wielded the sword
it danced in his hands
a swing of the mace
just amplified his grace

but it was the bow and arrow
where he reigned supreme
could get the whole world
shivering with terror
his arrows did not know
the meaning of error

to celebrate his graduation
the proud family decided to organise
a grand ceremony where
everyone was invited
princely or common
from all the corners of the world
and it was announced that
anyone coming could challenge
the prince to a duel
the award for defeating him
being his to be kingdom

and the day arrived
the stadium was bursting with crowd
everyone was eager
to have a glimpse of
the prince everyone had been talking about

the prince came
and with his skills at arms
mesmerized the crowd
the people watched in wonder

the sleight of his hands
it was as if
the god had descended the lands

and then the moment
everyone had been waiting for
the prince started walking to the pedestal
to claim the throne placed there
the crown to be bestowed on his head
the crown to prove he was the best

then suddenly a flurry of arrows
came flying obstructing his path
a wall of arrows to stop him
from reaching the crown
threatening him in front of all

the prince looked behind
wondering who can achieve
such a feat with such amazing speed
and saw a young man
at the entry gate

bare feet and bare chested
a simple bow in his hand
and a quiver with few arrows

a common in his appearance
dull colour and strongly built
his face was where his eyes got fixed
determination and ambition
writ so plainly there
it was as if
he was seeing the mirror

the thunderbolt stuck him
the emotion he never acknowledged
rising in his heart something new

SAURABH

it was the fear he never knew

THE SUN WARRIOR

he was a bastard
born out of wedlock
discarded in shame
found on sea waves

saved by fishermen
he got his parents
who lived by that sea
an elderly couple
who had lost their kid
to the same sea

the family was poor
used to live in a hut
the food was scarce
but there was no lack of love

resembling the shape of the sun
he had a birth mark on his back

it was as if someone had etched
his destiny on his skin with black

from the day he arrived
the fortunes started changing
once a sea village by the waves
it was now a prosperous sea port
bustling with ships and merchants
bringing in all the flourishing trades

he spent his childhood
playing on those shores
building castles with the sand
watching ships sail by
between the sea and the land

as the trade on the port
kept on increasing
the money and riches
kept on flowing
the kingsmen noticed that
and asked for a fat share
in all the earnings they had

the people said that it was unfair
but were told that it was the king
the god of all the lands and the seas
and they breathed because of him

the people still protested
against those unjust taxes
cowering down to the bullies
was something they never practised

the night came
and came the king's army
they burned the whole place down
and razed it to the ground

he got away unharmed
but lost everything that night
left with no family and friends
the lesson he learnt that night
to survive in this world
one needed might

he vowed to himself
that he would become
the mightiest man
in the world
and would use that might
to protect the weak
against the tyrants
of the world

so he set out on a journey
searching for a teacher
who could teach him to fight
one who could show him the light

but the world had always
been a cruel place
for a lowly born like him
everybody rejected him
the warrior's way was for the princes
and not for the people like him

dejected and humiliated
he wandered deep into the forests
came across a tribe
dwelling deep in the wild
kneeling down not to anyone
the nature being their queen
the tribal chief took pity on him
and promised to make him
the finest warrior anyone had seen

and so he began his training
the forest became his training arena
the birds and monkeys the spectators
lions and boars his duelling partners

he toiled day and night
with the flame blazing in his heart
he could uproot a tree with his bare hands
and a single arrow could pierce seven of them

the day finally came
when the chief told him
his training was complete
and he was now a warrior
no one would be able to defeat

he also told him about
the tidings wind had been carrying
about the warrior prince
and the open challenge
for anyone to defeat him

and he realised that moment
this was what he needed to do
to create a world of his liking
where the strong protected the weak

the seed got sown in his mind
and he decided
he needed to be the king

DRAWING FIRST BLOOD

the challenge was accepted
the rules were set
three rounds with three weapons
coming up first was the sword play

standing in the middle of arena
the sun warrior glanced all around
it was a full house
everyone cheering for the prince

he didn't mind that at all
soon they all would know
what he was all about

he looked at the man
he was about to face
trying to measure his confidence
but there was an

eerie calmness on this face

his stance was all eloquence
from head to the toe
he could not see any opening
how to strike down this foe

as they hovered each other in circles
his movements were so precise and guarded
this was a man of astute focus
he would have to rely
on the element of surprise

before he could make his move
the prince sprung and leaped towards him
his sword slashing and swishing in air
he parried the blows matching his speed
just managed to keep standing on his feet

the crowd joined in with a deafening roar
he had definitely lost the advantage of first move
the prince kept pushing him back
it was proving to be difficult to keep up with him

the man was brisk and swift
his body was amazingly flexible
dancing and arching
swaying like a loose string

he had to do something different
or it could be all over in minutes
the next blow was aimed at his shoulder
he raised the sword to block it
and then at last moment
left the shoulder unguarded
and jabbed the sword towards him

he missed his heart
as he had again moved quickly

but had drawn out his blood
he looked at his shoulder
it was bleeding from the cut he took

the two men paused for a second
their eyes met in that brief moment
he could see the surprise in them
and he knew he had the edge now

he lunged forward raining blows
kept pressing the prince
putting extra power in every blow
could sense the prince getting a bit slow

and then he saw the opening he has been waiting for
with quick strides approaching the prince
he swung the sword
with an intent to kill

but he again missed the mark
the prince had dodged the move
with a newfound speed
and with a swift action
changing the sword hand
made a slash catching on his wrist

the jolt of the strike
made him drop the sword
he was taken aback surprised
the prince had defeated him
and he has lost that bout

he heard the cheer again from the crowd
but there was something different about it
amid all the applauses for the prince
he could hear some voices
calling his name too

ACE OF THE MACE

the man was fearless
infringing insanity
wild spontaneous and unpredictable
his fighting style
certainly not the ordinary

for the second bout
he had chosen the heaviest mace
as if the limit of physical strength
was not even a concern at all
the prince looked at him grudgingly
the speed again he will have to rely upon

built like a mountain
lionhearted in his moves
throwing cautions to the winds
he was attacking giving it all in

blocking his thunderous blows
he couldn't help wondering
from where was all this anger coming from
certainly not the humiliation of his recent defeat
this was something more absolute and deep

a force so raw and vicious
he didn't know men can be so fierce
his next blow landed on his chest
and he was thrown off the ground
landed ten feet away and lost

the family was shocked and stunned
could not believe what they were seeing
but the crowd was on its feet
acknowledging the might of the man
bewitched by what he was doing

THE NEW KING

there were three key skills
a warrior needed to possess
speed might and accuracy
and hence three rounds
to establish the supremacy

the prince was certainly more faster
but the sun warrior had proved
to be the more mightier one
now to test their mastery at accuracy
the final round was a contest of archery

the organisers had set up
a series of challenges
they were asked to shoot down
targets stationery and movingtargets barely visible
targets behind some obstacles
so that they would have to

curve the arrows in flight

both of them were flawless
hitting the targets at ease
but then came the complexity
they had to take the aims
looking at the reflection
and then the targets became sounds
and they were blindfolded

the contest dragged on throughout the day
but a victor was nowhere in sight
as both of them were so precise
organisers also ran out of the tasks
and the round was declared a tie

the crowd thoroughly enthralled
by the feats of these two men
was now divided exactly in half
conveying their choice in applause

the council of judges huddled quickly
and came back to announce their decision
the prince was declared the winner
as the challenge was to defeat him
and the sun warrior had failed to do that

he was furious on how this was ending
but was also somewhat amused
this had been the way for justice to be served
this was the world where privileges were honoured

the prince was summoned to claim the throne
he started walking slowly towards the podium
thoughts racing through his mind
he had been taught that
the king was the best among men
and the best among men should be the king

but now having seen this man
he was not sure
and he had a doubt

standing on the podium and facing the crowd
he announced that he would not take the crown
there was still a lot for him to learn
and the crown was something he wanted to earn

so he would pass on the crown to the sun warrior
who had been proven worthy enough to be the king
and he would go on an exile of twelve years
to help him forget the royal blood in him
and then would also choose one year of anonymity
to prove he had lost his identity completely
and if he be discovered in that year of anonymity
then he would again go for twelve years of exile
followed by a year of anonymity again
till he had been forgotten as a prince

and then only he would come back to challenge the king
and to be proven that he was the best and the rightful king

the sun warrior was shocked and surprised
could not help admiring the integrity of this man
he walked up to him and asked him to
gift him his bow as a souvenir while he waited for him

he accepted the crown and was now the new king
and he declared to everyone in presence
that he would wait for these thirteen year to be over
and the prince to come and challenge him
till then he would rule the lands
along with the prince's bow beside him

THE DANCING PRINCESS

snow capped peaks of mountains
deep gorges carved out by rivers
hidden in the lap of nature
was a peaceful kingdom
where the princess was born

the king had two children
the son being the firstborn
he was supposed to be the next king
it had been like that since the beginning

but it was the princess
who had captured everyone's imagination
she had wisdom beyond years
she was like nature incarnated on earth

kind to the people
courage flowed in her veins
blessed with many talents

had eyes that could speak

the kind could see
the prodigy in her
and had left no stone unturned
to prepare her for the world

she had a busy schedule
classes throughout the day
but that one hour of dancing lessons
was what she kept looking forward to

dancing was where her heart was
or used to be some time back
now she had a dancing partner
who ruled her heart

she came a year back
and was exceptionally tall
but a wonderful dancer
and she was jealous of her
in the start

but as they danced together
she started knowing her
the grace in her movements
the dedication and focus she possessed
she was soon a dancer par excellence

the princess couldn't help falling for her
but she knew that she had many lovers
everyone was aware of her affairs
the men who used to visit her at nights
could never stop bragging about
their exploits in their nights

all that only stroked the flames in her
but she could never tell her
wondering what she would think of her

the woman was also not totally unaware
of the feelings the princess had for her
she could sense the burning desire
in those glances she kept stealing at her

she also felt the same
and wanted to reciprocate
but was afraid of the day
when princess would get to know
that she was no woman
but she was a warrior
born as a prince

the magic in the weed she had taken
was working wonders right then
but soon the effects would wear down
and she again would be a man
and would the princess still love her then

EYES OF A WOMAN

he had been to cites and villages
he had lived in the wild
he had spent time with sages
he had learnt from the wise

he had traveled far
both in body and mind
training them both
being both strong and kind

in his pursuit of excellence
he had mastered all arts
he could hold conversations
with an ignorant or
the one who taught

when having learnt everything
and wondering what to be done next
a eunuch reminded him that

it was only less than a half
he had seen in this world
and if he wanted to reign supreme
then he needed eyes of a woman
to see through the mysteries in this world

and then he had taken that weed
whose effects would last for more than a year
he would be transformed into a woman
something that could help him in his anonymity year

but he was unaware then
of the world he would see
of the love she would feel
it was the first time
she could feel her resolve wavering
she wanted to let go of her past
her ambitions and her aims
and dreamt of living on as a woman
revelling in her love till eternity ends

she was lost in thoughts of her princess
when she came charging to her
anger seething out from her eyes
the sun warrior had invaded their home
her father and brother had been defeated
and now the sun warrior would come
to claim his sovereignty on their lands
but the princess had not accepted the defeat yet
and was getting ready to march into the battle alone

in an instant and in that moment
the past had caught up again
the warrior in the woman stood up tall
and asked the princess to let her fight the war
and she would love to have her as the charioteer
the one who would guide her the ways

navigate the chariot through that hilly terrain
and carve the path to their win

the princess was surprised
but gladly accepted the offer
as she believed her words
with her love at her side
they would surely win the world

as they marched to the field
the woman was aware
that it was the last day
of her exile and the anonymity year
and she asked the princess
for one more favour
to not let her face the king
till the day was over

THEY SHOOK THE EARTH
WITH THEIR MIGHT

it had started raining
the light had gone dull
winds were picking speed
the clouds had started roaring

as they looked down onto the field
they could see the swarms of soldiers
spread across the horizon
some celebrating their victory
some heading back to their camps

as they reached the edge of field
the princess stood up and
sounded her conch shell
the woman fired the thunder arrows
to let the enemy know

the battle was not over yet
and they had not won it yet

the devastation they brought that day
many veterans had fallen that day
they shook the earth with their might
it was raining arrows that day

as they danced across the field
they were a sight to behold
moving around at a godly speed
soon the armies had started fleeing

the commanders rushed back to the camp
to let the king know
there were two women warriors in the field
who were creating havoc never seen before

the sun warrior was furious
he was promised by his advisors
that they would win the war
without a drop of blood been shed

but so many lives had been lost
and that too of his own people
he needed to end it swiftly
and with a heavy heart he got ready
and left for the field quickly

what he saw on the field
was mesmerising and spellbinding
two women warriors taking on the full might
of his armies and had brought them to their knees

they were moving so fast
that they were blur to his eyes
to have any chance to overpower them
he needed to first curtail their movement

so he raised his bow and shot a volley of arrows
the arrows aligning as walls to enclose
that part of field in a circle
with the king at one end
and the women warriors at the other

the chariot turned around to face the king
that was when the king first saw them
and was left dumbfounded by their beauty

were these the ones for whom
he had been searching for a while
the void in his life he had been feeling
and the reason he had been straying in life

an arrow hustled through brushing his left ear
the swishing sound jolted him back from his thoughts
that swing and smell of the arrow was so familiar
and the realisation dawned on him
the woman facing him with a bow in hand
was on one else but the warrior prince himself

their eyes met in that moment
the sun warrior glanced towards the sky
the sun had already set
the day was over
the exile was over
and he smiled back to the prince
breathing at last in relief

all the fighting had ceased
it was just those two in the field
a fierce battle was taking place
everyone stood there amazed
even time had stood still
to watch them that day

the princess was also a bit terrified

she had come down the chariot
and was watching the fight from some distance
doubting her lover even remembered her existence

the sun warrior had given his all
to match every strike from the prince
but he was a force unstoppable that day
it was as if the sun had chosen
to bless the prince that day

the sun warrior felt the terror up his spine
as the thought crossed his mind
it was the prince protecting the weak that day
and he crashed to the ground knowing
he could never win him that day

THE WAY OF THE KING

it was a bright new day
and there was a new king

he didn't sleep last night
his first in the palace
he had wanted to be the king
and now he could not wait
for what he wanted to do as the king

he spent the day talking to
his ministers and his kingsmen
and in the night he was on the streets
disguised as just another man

he learnt about how the things were
some from the ministers
and some from the streets
the place needed roads

and the people needed jobs

but first came the schools
which were not many
and teachers even less that a few
he visited nearby university
to recruit the teachers
convinced quite a few of them
saving the wisest to be his prime minister
the lone woman among those teachers

education was made mandatory
it needed to be a law so he made it a law
then he took care of the roads
connecting people across places
establishing trade across markets
prices were allowed to flow
as per the market forces
but for a few essential goods
the prices were regulated
a few things were made tax free
like books music and dance
or any other expression of speech and art
concerts were sponsored by him
encouraging people to attend at large

then came the office bearers
responsible for administration and judiciary
tests were conducted to assess the merit in them
and the conversations to seek out the dreamers among them

he had a lot to do
and he worked day and night
never took the time off for himself
and whatever spare time he could get
he was still spending it on the streets

the people seemed to be happy

living well and earning a living
but a fear was still there
as wars were still happening

he had reached to all the neighbouring kingdoms
had signed pacts of treaties with them
but once in a while
there was always an ambitious king
who wanted to be the king of the kings

so he had invested in a formidable army
to guard and protect the borders
also got them stationed in neighbourhoods
where his allies lacked the strength

the only direction left to secure
was up towards the north
the king there was a kind man
and had never worried about any war

all the efforts to get him convinced
to allow the troops to be on his lands
to help him ward off any aggression
had been treated with a smugly gesture

it was decided then
that the armies would march up north
to threaten the king with an attack
and seeing the might of armies on his door
the king would wise up to surrender

that was the decision
he was still regretting that night
the wisdom he saw earlier
was cloaked in the insecurity of might

and it had to be destiny
that it was the warrior prince again
who had come back

to wake him up in that rain

he didn't sleep that night
waiting eagerly for the next day
when the prince would arrive
and it would get decided in the ring
whether he was good enough to be the king

WHO SHOULD BE THE KING?

the princess had also come along
and had convinced the prince
that she would be the judge
if the sun warrior would allow that

as they reached the arena
it was again a full house
everyone was cheering for their king
no one could even recognize the prince

the sun warrior came forward
and greeted them with respect
he returned the bow to the prince
and asked them how to begin

he agreed on the princess

being the judge and
setting up the rules

all three of them
moved to the centre of arena
where everyone could see them

the princess told everyone that
the selection of the king would be
basis the answers they would provide
to the five questions she would ask

the sun warrior being the ruling king
would get to answer first
to the first three questions
which would be asked
and the prince would answer first
the remaining two questions to be asked

with every one in the crowd witnessing them
the princess started with her questions

Who am I?

You are neither the body you possess nor the knowledge you seek. You are the consciousness you share with the world.

I am the time and the being. I am the present with a known past and an unknown future.

Why am I born?

You are born as you were wanted. Someone in the world needed you to be born.

I am born to contribute. I am born to take the journey forward.

What is the ultimate truth?

Truth is a perspective and no one truth is truer than the other truth. Day and night, good and bad and truth and lie are all equal truths. There is no one ultimate truth.

Death is the one ultimate truth. Whatever is born will one day die.

Then what is destiny?

My thoughts and my actions are my destiny. The law of nature is cause and effect. And that law is my destiny.

The destiny is the road to our future. We create this road on every step as we travel on it.

Who should be the king?

The wisest and the kindest among people should be the king. One who has a kind heart and the most knowledge on the ways of the world should be entrusted with the caring of the people.

You should be the king. The voice inside you should be your king guiding you on the path of your life. And if one voice needs to represent all of our voices together, then it should be the voice of the one which echoes the most with all the voices.

the princess nodded to him

and declared to the crowd
it would be the sun warrior
who would be their king

the sun warrior looked at the prince and said
he could have shared with him
and both of them could have been the kings

the prince smiled
and replied back
he dreamt of being the best among men
but he dreamt of being the king

Acknowledgement

Many thanks to medium.com and artstation.com to bring this book into reality.

My heartfelt thanks to all the artists whose imaginations have helped in the imagery for my words. Credits for the images used in the book

Title : R Kamalakkannan
https://www.artstation.com/artwork/dey01

The warrior prince : Bhavin Mehta
https://www.artstation.com/artwork/rbAeE

The sun warrior : Alok Joshi
https://www.artstation.com/artwork/PmWbo1

Drawing first blood : Vamchi Vams
https://www.artstation.com/artwork/w60o19

Ace of the mace : Bhavin Mehta
https://www.artstation.com/artwork/qAvBW2

The new king : Chandra Sekhar Poudyal

https://www.artstation.com/artwork/Oybm06

The dancing princess : M Arief Russanto
https://www.artstation.com/artwork/lXNJ5

Eyes of a woman : Simon Raskina
https://www.artstation.com/artwork/xzqkzO

The shook the earth with their might : Binu Balan
https://www.artstation.com/artwork/aDPPz

The way of the king : Shanmugavel Velu
https://www.artstation.com/artwork/zZ5gL

Who should be the king? : Aleksandr Kuskov
https://www.artstation.com/artwork/w3Qqg

9 7 9 8 6 8 0 8 6 5 3 0 9